Interracial Fantasy BBC Bundle

Black Friday, Volume 6

Dylan Dudebro et al.

Published by The Cream Team Publishing, 2024.

INTERRACIAL FANTASY BBC BUNDLE

First edition. February 9, 2024.

ISBN: 979-8224506408

Written by Dylan Dudebro et al..

Table of Contents

The Intern: Jamal stays late at Work to Help His Boss

By: Suzi Slay

I was spending another late night at the office. This project is going to kill me or get me fired. I wouldn't be close to making our launch date if not for Jamal. Painfully, I must admit, at first, I thought he was a product of affirmative action. I guessed he was only hired because of his skin color, not his brains. While an undergraduate, he played football, so he couldn't be that smart, right? I believed his high grades were the product of manipulation from the athletic office. Acceptance into an elite graduate school was the byproduct of the inflated grades, taking a spot from a worthy applicate, and he parlayed his position into an internship. In my mind, this was all true.

I was wrong, so wrong. It was the opposite. The other interns graduated from elite high school prep programs at elite undergraduate universities and are now enrolled in elite graduate schools. They hail from prestigious families and feel entitled to be here. Jamal grew up poor, paid for school via an athletic scholarship, and still had higher grades than the other interns. No, I want him on my team next year after completing his second year of grad school. He had an energy to him I fed off. I never had a direct report with that effect on me.

The Director of Project Management, Lisa, tried to steal him from my workgroup. That whore can't help herself. She almost creamed herself on his first day. I stopped her advances quickly. Lisa wasn't the only one.

2

I had to beat off the other interns and some of the junior members of the team from flirty with him all day. It was almost a full-time job stopping an HR incident from occurring.

Jamal was taller than most men, had sexy dreads that he put into a ponytail, and wore tailored suits that gripped his muscular body. An infectious personality ensured he was central to most office discussions. He smelled of cologne and cocoa butter. The man was stunning. If I didn't have a husband, I would have been in the running to harass him, too. Not to marry him but to test-drive what was under his hood. *Who wouldn't want a spin with a sports car like that?*

Neck Pain

I popped two more painkillers because of pain in my neck. I officially hit the age when stuff hurts because you slept on it wrong or the universe was saying fuck you to me this week. My body felt like it was breaking down from the stress and pressure of the project. Mentally, I didn't have much left. I received a text from my husband, once again furious, that I wasn't coming home until late. He flung insults at me as the marriage fell off a cliff. I wish he were more supportive of me like the other husbands of working women. I hope he will understand how much he negatively affected my health one day.

"Are you Okay," Jamal said in a deep baritone voice that no man his age should have. A voice that powerful should only belong to platinum soul singers, presidents, or God voice-overs, not interns. Its bass tickled my soul. I gathered myself to look at him. Hoping the pain lines on my face didn't show.

"Is it that obvious?" I said. Showing weakness was rare for me in the office, but my neck felt like thirty people were performing the *Irish River Dance* on it. "My neck is killing me," I explained. Rubbing it was helping a little, but the painkillers were losing effectiveness by the day. If this continues for a week, I may be on bed rest. I continued to rub the sore spot in the hope of relief.

"It wasn't obvious until you yelled fuck and grabbed your neck," he explained. I didn't even realize I cursed out loud. I felt embarrassed that I did that. I am a girl boss, but I felt like a little girl who needed her daddy. "Do you need some help with that? I used to get stingers a lot when I played football. Our trainers worked the knots out all the time. I know all the secrets, trust me. You work hard enough. Having neck pain is wrong. Come one, and let me help you out."

On the drive home, I identified this as the turning point, the moment I should have said, "No, thank you," and kept working. As you guessed by now, I didn't. I said, come over here, Jamal, and rub my shoulders. I am such an idiot sometimes. Okay, back to the story.

TURNING POINT

Jamal walked over and placed his strong hands on my shoulder. Ripples of pain relief emanated from the stable hands. Both thumbs pressed the bottom of the neck and moved in a circular pattern. "You will feel some pressure and a little pain at first, but in the end, you will love it, "he whispered. I suddenly felt better and a little of something else. At first, I struggled to place the feeling because it had been so long. I was horny. That young man pierced the wall I put up with his mighty hand and fingers.

The palms of his hands rubbed against my blazer, so I pushed them off my shoulders. Jamal's fingers expanded across my neck and shoulders. At first, the friction felt tremendous, but I began to chafe. My skin was dry from a long day in the office. I reached into my designer purse on my desk and retrieved the lotion. Jamal's hands didn't stop when I moved; he followed my movements to the bag and back into the chair. He was determined not to let go for a second. Cupped hands entered my line of sight to receive the lotion. I squirted it three times.

"Don't worry, I will get that later," Jamal said.

"Get what?" He laughed but did not answer. The boss wanted to know the meaning of the statement. I ask the questions and my direct reports answer. That was the way of things. I waited thirty seconds for him to volunteer the information before asking him, "When will you get it?" Once again, he laughed. I laughed, too, completely missing the joke, but I didn't want to feel left out. Maybe he made a sports reference or something that I didn't understand.

"Do you know what I like about you, Melissa? You get straight to the point. At first, I wondered if the vibes I was getting from you were real. First, you asked me to work late. Next, you cock-blocked my conversions with female interns and junior team members. Lastly, when Lisa threw herself at me, you stopped her. I thought you might want me. But right now, you finally gave me the sign." Jamal's hands moved down the v-neck shirt. My eyes tracked the tips of his fingers. I finally saw the lotion that missed his hands and landed on my breast. His hand slid over the cream and continued into the front of my shirt. Outstretched fingers entered my bra.

Holy shit, what the fuck is he doing, and how is this happening right now? The world crashed around me — clarity of the events that led to the situation. I made him work late. I cock-blocked him from the younger women at work. Shit, I even asked him to rub my shoulders, a no-no in corporate America. Then, like a whore, I squirted fucking lotion on my tits. *Melissa, what are you doing?* Get your life together. I froze for the first time I could remember. Large hands gripped my breast. Once again, I should have stood up and ended it.

I Should Stop Him

My subconscious, let's call her Connie, wanted this. That bitch Connie arranged the events and then sprung the surprise. I bet she was the one that missed the last squirt of lotion. Connie dressed me in five-inch heels and tight pants. I imagine she encouraged me to shave my private area that morning, eat pineapples for breakfast and lunch, and spray perfume everywhere. The chain of events was too much of a coincidence. Connie, my subconscious, set me up. That is my story, and I am sticking to it.

The pleasure from my breast rippled from my nipples outward. I could feel my pussy getting wet, my mouth watered, and my toes were curling. My mind raced to find a way to stop what was happening, but my body wanted it to continue under Connie's guidance. Goosebumps exploded when he kissed the back of the neck. I let out a moan when his tongue reached the edge of my ear. My mind was telling me no, but my body was saying yes. *Melissa, if you don't stop this right now, my brain said. You have a husband and kids.* Connie told my rational brain to shut the fuck up and we will deal with that later. Right now, we had large hands playing with our love muffins.

My internal conflict raced as fast as my heart was beating. A nibble on the top of the ear sent me into a frenzy. Long fingers gripped and tugged on my nipples. With all my willpower left, I stood to face Jamal. I had to explain to him that it was a mistake, it wasn't his fault, and we could forget the entire thing. I wouldn't treat him differently, and it wouldn't be weird between us. Jamal released my shoulders, feeling my urge to stand, so he allowed it. I stood facing away from him as I gathered my courage. Jamal pushed the chair to the side, pulled me closer, one hand on my hip, grinding his hard cock against my ass, and slipping one hand back on my breast from under my blouse. I couldn't see the cock, but it had to be massive. It moved rhymical between my ass cheeks. Those lush lips returned to the back of my neck. Damn it, Jamal. You were supposed to wait for me to tell you to stop.

"Too late bitch," said Connie.

I tried to speak, but I could only let out a gasp followed by a moan. With tremendous skill, Jamal unbuttoned my suit pants with one hand. *Okay, stop him now before he reaches your wet pussy.* Too late. My head leaned back onto his chest — moans of pleasure echoing in the office. Fingers danced under my panties. The well-lotioned hand found my clit with ease after splitting moist pussy lips. My clit poked out, eager for his embrace and excited to be in use. Fingers slid in and out of my soaking wet womanhood. His middle finger was more massive than some penises I had; my limp dick husband's penis could not even rival it.

I gripped tightly with my pussy lips, a technique I learned trying to spice up my shitty marriage, but it slid in and out with ease because I was so wet. Jamal's left hand was under my blouse, lifting my bra above my breast, exposing them for better access. They bounced as I twitched from the pleasures below. He cupped, flicked, and massaged my funbags with equal attention. Jamal's mahogany skin clashed with my pale breast. Pink nipples exploded outward, yearning for another flick or rub. I couldn't form words with my mouth - only moans. Fingers angled perfectly to rub my g-spot, Jamal continued, and I squeezed my lips. It only took a minute for my little used pussy to burst. I convulsed in Jamal's powerful arms, biceps squeezing my frail body and lifting me off the ground. I tried to break free and fall to the ground in orgasmic shame, but he held me tight, moving in and out faster to ensure I exploded. I twitched and convulsed for thirty seconds or so before he spoke.

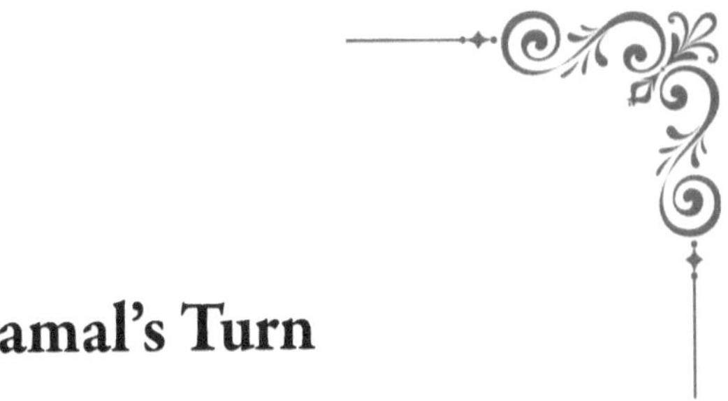

Jamal's Turn

"**A**re you warmed up yet?" he whispered in my ear. Shit, I couldn't remember the last time I felt that, if ever. Jamal dropped my spent body in the chair and spun it around to face him. "Unbutton it," he ordered. Without a thought, I unlatched his belt and then unzipped the pants. Connie was in control now, and Melissa was just a passenger on the romp with the intern.

A mahogany monster cock flopped out. I heard legends of monster cocks, like the one pointing at me, only mentioned at bachelorette parties, drunken girl's nights, or in obscene books, never in polite society. It was like I found the cock version of Bigfoot. I couldn't believe what I was seeing. It hypnotized me. No, better yet, it dickmatized me.

"Holy shit." I reached out to touch it cautiously like it was a snake or another dangerous animal.

"That's what you wanted, isn't it, Melissa? A fat black cock in your little white mouth. I know you don't get this at home." Jamal was correct; I didn't get this at home but would get it today.

Let's run down the facts. I had a little white mouth, check. Jamal had a big black dick, check. I also had a nicely-shaven pink pussy that called for attention. Connie must have done that. Should I suck it and let him cum in my mouth? Pull it out and make him cum all over my sensitive breast? No, I've gone this far; I must go all the way. I wanted it inside me, that is, if it fits.

I grabbed his fat cock and stroked it once. A small drop of precum was on the head. I stoked it again to see if more would form. The pure white color was a stark contrast against the dark skin of his dick. My hand didn't even come close to fitting around the girth. I needed both hands to handle the beautiful, long, dark monster. Veins pulsed along the shaft under my palm, and I stroked.

I jagged it a little faster, and I grew in amazement with each stroke. It smelled wonderful, a mix of cologne and cocoa butter, just like the rest of him. My tongue licked the precum on the tip of his penis. It was sweet, like chocolate. I could get the first four inches inside on the first push. He moved his hips, face fucking me slowly, with more of his girth going inside my hungry mouth. Silvia dripped from my chin and his dick onto my shirt and exposed tits. It glistened on Jamal's cock. He rammed it in and out, no longer gentle, making me gag at times. I thought it was going to hit the back of my throat. I couldn't even fit half of it in my mouth, but I tried. My mother didn't raise a quitter, but if she could see this, I imagine she wouldn't have pushed her little angel so hard never to give up.

You Will Feel Some Pressure

Jamal picked me up and placed me on my desk. He pulled my right leg out of my suit pants. With force, the intern ripped my panties clean off with one tug. My cleanly shaven wet pussy was now exposed, nothing stopping his manhood from claiming the prize and getting what he wanted from me.

"Put it in," he ordered. I nodded like a nasty schoolgirl. I grabbed the monster, wet it with my saliva, and pulled it closer to my national treasure. I said a short prayer for my little lips because she would need it. "You will feel some pressure and a little pain at first, but in the end, you will love it." He repeated the line from before. This motherfucker had planned for this moment, and I was glad that he did.

The tip went in, exploring the resistance and developing a plan of attack. Dripping from spit and my Niagara Falls wet nookie, lubrication wasn't the problem. My tight, barely used vagina was the problem. It stretched, trying to take the monster, but the old girl wouldn't quit. Slowly, it went in more, the massive head filling up my insides, moving against my spot.

"You like that black dick, don't you? Take it like a good little girl." I gasped as he shoved it inside. It was so deep. It filled every available inch of the inside of my mommy maker, the veins on the cock rubbing against my sugar walls and tingling my insides. It only took a couple of thrusts before I came again. My spasms knocked staplers and pens off the desk as my arms flailed. Jamal picked me up and carried me. Both arms under my knees, holding in the air, pounding my pussy with his thick penis. It was a surreal moment for me to see my toes next to his head, one in a shoe and one out. I used the open-toed expensive shoes to tease my boss, who I knew had a foot fetish. Now, I watched them clack against the side of his head as gravity worked my insides. His balls were smacking against the bottom of my naughty zone. We locked eyes, and I could speak for the first time during this.

"Harder." Why the fuck did I say that? Connie was up to her old tricks again. She wanted it all, and now I knew I would get all he had. I never wanted to know what it was like to be pummeled by a black man; today, I was going to find out. He responded, turning up the speed and power. The tip of the penis hit my cervix; it went so deep. Jamal's hips smashed my ass and leg, creating slapping sounds. We locked eyes, and I was to speak once more, "Cum inside me."

What? Why would I say that? Fucking Connie is trying to get me killed or pregnant. I felt his penis convulse for ten seconds until it exploded. It felt like a thousand gallons of his warm seed filled my baby maker. The feeling sent my little lips into a frenzy. I came again, bucking in his arms and shaking. His girth continued to pulse. I squeezed my labia once more to ensure I got every last drop out of that amazing cock. He held me, both of us panting, before he let me down.

There I was. Cum dripped down my right leg. The other leg still had the pantsuit leg up to my hip with my heel on. My breast hung under my pulled-up shirt - dripping with spit from my chin. My hair was a disaster, and my glasses bent at an odd angle and were not functional. I was cum dazed and confused but entirely sexually satisfied.

"That's all for today, Jamal. You can go home." I had to scramble for my back clothes and quickly put them on before someone found me half-naked. After that day, my neck didn't hurt anymore. I guess he fucked the pain away. We hooked up a couple of times before he went back to school.

The company offered him a position at the firm, but he turned it down and took another job. I cried for a week. Last week, he texted me asking if I was attending an industry conference. I wasn't going when he sent me the text, but I was going five minutes later. I will see him again in two weeks, and I can't wait to see him.

Cuffed: A Naughty White Milf Takes Advantage

By: Dylan DudeBro

Gloria laughed harder than she should at the situation unfolding in her house. It was not funny, but it was. Maybe it was the whiskey sour that sparked this bought of laughter. Keisha, her best friend, handcuffed her son but forgot the key at home. The Friendsgiving always had a theme, and this year was superhero-themed. Keisha arrived dressed as Batgirl, complete with handcuffs. During a family dispute, the woman put the handcuffs on her son. The confused Batgirl believed it was the trick cuffs but soon realized they were the authentic ones she and her husband would use when they wanted to spice it up.

Tommy tried to free himself but couldn't. Even though the massive six-foot-six-inch man cosplayed as the black panther, he couldn't break the cuffs. Keisha, mortified, jumped into her car and returned to her house to get the key to free her son. In the meantime, Gloria, who wore superhero cosplay, laughed at Tommy in the kitchen. The twenty-one-year-old young man took the jokes but wanted

"I am sorry, Tommy. This is too funny," said Gloria as she tried to compose herself. The older woman eyed her friend's mature son. Swollen muscles flexed and spasmed from trying to break free of the cuffs, and she noticed how mature his body had become for the first time. It's not polite to stare, but they were laughing at the situation in the kitchen.

Gloria's eyes raked over the tight cosplay costume as it hugged his body. The thin and cheap fabric left very little to the imagination, but she was imagining anyway. A broad chest stretched the material not meant for a body of his size. Nipples poked into the uniform, threatening to tear. Gloria pretended to fiddle with her straw, lowering her head and eyes. The dark material gripped the hidden six or possibly eight-pack—a sexy "V" lead straight to the grand prize. The material gripped his lower body and crotch. For the first time, she could see an outline of his manhood. The size of it couldn't be right, could it? Embarrassed by her actions, the older woman pulled her gaze away and continued to calculate the measurements taken.

"Gloria, how many times have I asked her if she had the key? At least ten. She once cursed me out because she thought I was calling her stupid. Here I am, handcuffed in my mother's friend's house," he joked. His words snapped her attention. Tommy always had a crush on Gloria. As a man in his sexual prime, he wished he was still handcuffed but on a bed with his mom's friend naked. Tommy's eyes wandered to her well-maintained body. The naught mommy had the zipper on her costume pulled down to expose her luscious breasts. Tommy's imagination continued to expand and take in the amazing sight.

Gloria's eyes shot from his manhood to the face. His brown eyes darted away instantly as he pretended to look at something behind her. It seems she wasn't the only one checking out the opposite sex. She caught Tommy gazing at her exposed breasts. The milf awkwardly smiled and pulled her hair over her near ear in a nervous tick. The kitchen was quiet, but the new sexual tension remained.

"Gloria...I need your help. I need to go to the bathroom," said Tommy. Gloria burst out laughing again. Tommy started laughing and then began to hop around like a five-year-old. The magnitude of the request didn't hit her until the logistics were apparent. Tommy couldn't use his hands, and she would need to undress him to help. That sort of activity could not occur in the basement or 1st-floor bathroom. Too many people were moving about and using those bathrooms. She thought about calling his dad, but the noise from the men in the basement meant that would probably not happen. Gloria searched for ideas and then came up with a solution.

"Fine, come this way. I will take you to the primary bathroom," she said. Gloria grabbed under the arm and escorted him from the kitchen, up the stairs, and into the primary bedroom. From the bedroom, they walked into the opulent primary bathroom. Grey floors, dark word fixtures, and white marble signified that the renovations from last year were not cheap.

Tommy walked to the toilet and stood in front of it. Gloria was still laughing until it finally set in what "Helping" meant. A twang of guilt ran down her spine. Gloria put down the drink on the sink and moved closer to Tommy. Upon inspecting the outfit, she didn't see a zipper in the front but one in the back. He couldn't go to the bathroom even if she unzipped the costume.

Helping Hand

"**I** think I need to cut a hole," Gloria said. The building pressure forced a noticeable dance. She retrieved a pair of scissors from the drawer. Gloria got on her knees and grabbed the material. For the first time, she felt his girth. The milf needed to know where he was in the material. The cock underneath sparked to life when she tried to separate the material from his manhood. Gloria coughed at the sudden growth. In an instant, she was sober. "We never talk about this. Do you understand me? We never speak of this to anyone."

"I understand," he said. Tommy couldn't believe what was happening. The excitement of Gloria being this close to him, and to it. The excitement was driving a horniness previously unknown. The only thing Tommy wanted was for Gloria to touch it. The memory alone would provide decades of spank bank material. "I know how to keep secrets."

Gloria smiled and put one finger to her lips in the universal signal to be quiet. Pale fingers worked to separate the material from the man. The bulge grew larger and larger. Tommy wasn't even fully erect and was larger than her husband. The milf's thoughts traveled back twenty years to college when she hooked up with Sun State's all-time leading rusher Kaytron Baller. It was the last time she felt something this big. Silvia drenched the inside of her mouth with the memory of taking that big boy in her mouth. Gloria poked a hole into the thin fabric, eager to see what Tommy had under the uniform.

Tommy felt the soft hand of his mom's friend on his cock. Tommy tried momentarily to keep his black panther at bay, but he now understood that was impossible. He dreamed for the better part of the last decade of Gloria holding, sucking, and riding his magic stick, and today one of the three was happening. Tommy now was trying to impress the milf. Her eyes hadn't left his bulge since she started, and he could tell that she may be as excited as he was. She made a hole in the material, and Tommy held his breath for the next steps.

Gloria placed the scissors on the vanity and used her fingers to open the hole more. Curious fingers reached inside until they touched the pride of Wakanda. Tommy was bouncing more and more by the moment. Both hands went inside the hole to grab his cock and balls to pull them out. Holding the enormous cock sent her into overdrive. Her pale hand stroked it once to experience the entire length.

"Gloria, I really have to go," said Tommy. Gloria had many unfulfilled fetishes, but a golden shower wasn't one of them. She lifted the toilet seat, stood up, moved to the side, and aimed the shaft with both hands. The aim was true, and cosplaying Tommy fired into the toilet.

Tommy felt the pleasure of releasing the built-up body fluid. He pushed for it to come out, and the relief was terrific. The other fantastic thing was the pale hands gripping his hard cocomelon. The milf stroked the cock in an attempt to help him go to the bathroom, but it was helping him get harder instead. As the pressure of the piss ended, the pleasure of the slight stroking increased.

If you had told Gloria this morning that she would be double-fisting her best friend's son meat, she would have slapped you. It swelled in her hand as he finished. Neither spoke because they understood something was happening, and they possibly crossed a line. She held the black mamba in awe. *Was I wrong? Was he wrong?* She thought. Her husband was in the house, and she was holding another man's cock. Outside of that one Miami girlstrip fifteen years ago, she has been faithful.

"Stroke out the drips," said Tommy. He didn't know if the plow for her to stroke him more would work. If Gloria hadn't been interested in her work, she may have seen the sweat dripping from his forehead when he asked. Gloria stroked it several times to get out the drips without questioning Tommy. The dark brown cock pumped inside her pale hands until it was fully erect. Curious, the strokes continued after the last drips, but Tommy wasn't complaining.

"One second. Let me clean it," said Gloria. She put warm water on a hand towel and walked to the mighty meat. The towel cleaned the drips away before it was tossed into the towel bin. Gloria returned to the cock, and gripped it again with two hands before stroking. "I have to make sure I got it all out."

"Do you like it?" Tommy asked. The words hung in the air. Gloria did like it. The mamba DICKmatized her. Every voice in her head screamed for her to stop what she was doing. She didn't answer those calls but kept stroking it. Gloria told herself she would stop in a second, but only after seeing how big it got. She had already put her hand on his cock to help him, so the damage was done. It wouldn't hurt to hold it for a little longer.

"Tommy. I don't know how to say this, but...your cock is amazing," said Gloria. The hefty weight and girth fixated the mommy.

"Thank you," Tommy replied. The young man was processing the momentum of the events. How far could this go? How much could he do? He knew this was wrong on one level, but on the other level, he wanted this more than any pursuit of a female in his life. "I don't think I can go back to the party with my cock out. Especially like this," said Tommy. Gloria slowly raised her gaze to his. The two locked eyes and traded a conversation of lust.

"Sit down, and I will get you a pair of shorts," she said. The entire trip into his room to get the shorts, her mind could only focus on the beast in the other room. Her lady bits were eager and ready and calling for Tommy. Gloria slowly retrieved the shorts, hoping that when she returned, the monster would have returned to the liar. She had fun and would joke about the experience one day, but now the fun was over. Gloria continues to convince herself out of the thoughts she had and the experience of the previous.

Do You Want My Help

Gloria walked into the bathroom with the shorts. Tommy sat on the toilet, and his cock reached for the sky. A small drip of precum flowed down the shaft. Gloria wasn't built to handle this type of excitement. The last of her resistance to him was crumbling. The desire to ride that panther grew by the second. She walked into the bathroom, shut the door, and locked it.

"Damn, Tommy. Will it go down?" asked Gloria. The milfs eyes keenly fixated on the exposed appendages. Gloria thought her heart would explode. The pounding would break a rib if he didn't stop. She licked her lips as she slowly walked to the twenty-one-year-old.

"I don't know. It better go down. If mom comes back and I am rock hard, she is going to kill both of us," he said. His eyes pleaded with her to help with the problem before them. He needed her to piece it together and devise the solution independently.

"If you cum it will go down, right?" Gloria didn't know why she asked the answer but assumed her pussy asked it.

"Yes," Tommy said, drawing out the answer.

"Do you want my help?" she asked. Gloria began to panic. Was she going to let her emotions get the better of her? This doesn't seem right. "It is okay to say no. We can figure something else out if it is too much. I don't even know why I asked. We shouldn't do this."

"Do what? I need your help, Gloria. Please help me," pleaded Tommy. The anticipation threatened to cause a heart attack. The excitement of Gloria touching him and making him climax was fap fuel.

"Okay. I will help you and, in turn, help us. Remember, we don't talk about what happens here. You said that you could keep secrets. Well, this is a big one," said Gloria. She got to her knees in front of Tommy and grabbed the big black cock. The right hand gripped the base, and the left gripped the top before switching. In unison, she jerked it. Disbelief and amazement conflicted inside her. The black mamba was a two-hander. She jerked the massive cock, but it was too dry to get the wanted motion.

Gloria decided to save them from her best friend's retribution. Silva dripped from her mouth, and she put it on the head of the monster. *Here goes nothing.* The jaw opened as wide as it could to take the head. Silvia ran down the shaft to be collected by the right hand. The slickness dripped down to his balls. The left hand cradled the balls and played with them.

"I am only doing this to help us, okay? I only want to help you," Gloria said as she tried to convince Tommy and herself. She took both hands off the massive monster, but her mouth kept it in place. The hands gripped the front zipper and pulled it down. Unlike Tommy's costume, the outfit had a long zipper in the front. Two yanks on the zipper freed it to fall. The naughty helper pulled the zipper down her ladybits. Mature breasts spilled from the costume, the right hand returned to the stiff rod, and the other hand went to her lady bits.

The hand played with the sensitive joystick, causing a moan to vibrate his member. Tommy bit his lip and cursed silently. Her mouth took over for the hand until he was ready to cum. The taste of the precum drove her wild. Gloria deserved to experience it.

Gloria lost herself as she sucked and played with herself, but she couldn't take the entire thing. One finger slipped inside herself before being joined by a second finger. The exercise warmed up the milf muffin. Three fingers dove inside her wet wookie as she tried to prepare herself to receive Tommy's throat smasher. The fingers dripped wet, and Gloria felt that maybe she could handle the massive cock. She pulled away from the hard cock with her spit dripping from her mouth and the shaft. The woman stood up and pulled the zipper to the rear, exposing herself.

"What are you doing?" asked Tommy, but they both knew what she was doing.

"Helping," she said. "Do you still want my help? I mean, I could put the shorts on instead."

"No. I want your help. I have always wanted your help. I dreamed about this," said Tommy. Something about the statement made her pause and blush. Deep down, she knew he would steal a glimpse of her. Teenagers have notorious bad eye discipline, but the attention she received felt good. "Put it inside, please it in."

Gloria lost the ability to stop herself when she heard him plead for her. The lust took over. The dark brown boomstick touched her tight little pink marvel. She lowered herself onto it, and her spit and wet lips did the rest. Once inside, it stretched her to the limits. She moaned after only the tip went inside. She leaned forward, putting her breast into his face and guiding one nipple into his mouth—another stroke and another inch deeper. The ocean Gloria once called her vagina dripped wet from the engagement with the monster. Tommy groaned as Wakanda's pride went to work.

"Tommy, it's okay. I am just helping. That's all. Just helping," she said as her love muffin took three more inches of the monster. Gloria put both hands against the wall behind him. Moans of pleasure echoed in the bathroom. The huge mamba worked inside slowly. Jealously she hated her friend for having a cock this nice attached to her son. She could never tell Keisha about it, but Keisha probably had the older version with Tommy's father. Gloria never had anything like this before. This was her only moment to have it, and she would take full advantage.

"Damn, Gloria, you are tight," said Tommy. He didn't know what to expect from a woman of her age. Most college girls were tight, but for some reason, he thought milfs were loose. He was wrong. Another thing was happening, too. Her insides were gripping his shaft. Tommy heard about this technique before but thought it was nonsense. Well, today, he was being taught lessons. Unfortunately, the class would not last long. The milf motion was pulling the orgasm from him at a speed that he had never encountered.

The inner freak dormant inside Gloria rocked back and forth on the wood. She picked up the pace and put one hand on his shoulder to steady herself. The whole ten inches was going all the way in. She could feel it touch places inside of her that had never been touched before. A stream of curses erupted in a hushed tone with every stroke.

"Wakanda forever," she shouted and continued to ride. She bounced faster and faster until her slick snatch was able to take it all. It gushed and gobbled it all. Somehow, it hurt like hell but felt amazing at the same time. The dichotomy confused and enticed her to keep going. Which one would win out?

"I am going to cum," Gloria said.

"I am going to cum," Tommy said.

Gloria didn't hear a word he said in her current state of bliss. She bounced on it until both erupted at the same time. The chocolate milk splashed into her cock riding cereal. Shocked by the sudden splash, her body went into full orgasm. Gloria leaned forward and hugged Keisha's son tightly as the ripples of pleasure splashed against the hot rockets firing inside. Tommy's cock twitched with every explosion, and Gloria's lady bits clamped down on his member. Each one of the movements sent a gallon of goo inside. They both dove into a pool of ecstasy.

Gloria leaned forward, breathing heavily and trying to process that Tommy just exploded inside her unprotected pussy. She stopped taking birth control when her husband got a vasectomy. Now, eager young sperm raced to capture the prize. That was a problem or another day, though. The moment would last a little longer as the milf ground the last waves of her orgasm and the last squirts of his. They shared a long kiss full of tongue and heavy breathing.

"I am back," said Keisha. The forgetful mom walked into the kitchen. Gloria and her husband stood in the kitchen mocking her son, Tommy. She quickly unlocked the handcuffs that she put on her son. "Sorry, baby."

"Don't worry about it, mom. Gloria took care of me," said Tommy with a large smile. Gloria laughed and took another sip of her drink.

Jazzy Jugs: A Hucow Tale

By: Egirl Emily

I love New Orleans. When I could travel to a work conference, I jumped. The Jazz scene in New Orleans is impressive. My father was well-trained on the trumpet. I spent many years in the city when my father performed. A lot of my early childhood was spent here in the back alley bars, listening to some of the greatest musicians in the world. Pictures of him with the greats lined our walls growing up. I feel closer to him and my early memories in the city. The last time I was in town, I didn't have the opportunity to visit the legendary underground jazz bar called Voodoo Lounge, but this time, I was going to correct that mistake. As a kid, this was the only bar that didn't let me stay past eight o'clock. I always thought it was because of violence, but the last time I was in town, I heard a different story, and I wanted to check it out.

The small bar was almost at capacity on a Tuesday night. I sat at a small wooden table and ordered a whiskey on the rocks. The first sip burned, but the caramel hints of the dark liquor mixed well with the cigar smoke. My red cocktail dress and open-toed high heels shoes matched the surroundings, but my red hair and pale skin stood out. Afros, braids, and locks were the prominent hairstyles worn by the women and men inside the bar. With that said, I felt at home in the Jazz club. I fit, and they all knew it.

The performances moved my soul, and the drinks amplified my enjoyment. Multiple bands played, each with a unique style unfamiliar to my seasoned ears. At times, the dance floor was filled with people dancing. At other times, everyone sat and admired the trumpet, saxophone, or piano playing of the veterans. It was by far the best jazz club I visited in years and maybe ever. I took another sip of the double whiskey on the rocks. Its burn lessened due to the mild intoxication. I was at peace here. No more rigors of work, men, and everything life tossed my way daily. No, all I needed was the whiskey and the music in here. Peace.

One more sip and I will go back to my room, I told myself for the tenth time. I knew I would stay until the end, but I had to trick myself into believing I would leave early. I don't care how tired I am at the conference tomorrow. One by one, couples left the Jazz bar. We didn't have this in the Midwest, so I would soak up every beat, sound, and song until they kicked me out. A dark-skinned musician with a pinstriped suit, bowtie, and a newsboy hat approached me. He was in his early thirties and highly familiar. A broad smile across his face indicated I was familiar to him, too. I smiled in return, though I didn't know him or his intentions.

He stopped at the edge of my table, his voice baritone, "Glad you finally made it, Irene. I was wondering if you were going to come or not?" I searched for the face, and I was lost. "I met you at the Victory Lounge on Bourbon three or four months ago," he said. My eyes widened. This was the man who told me about the jazz bar. That time, he only wore blue jeans and a t-shirt, making it hard to place the man. He was also with a childhood friend of mine. *What was his name again? Oh yeah.*

"Joseph?"

"That's me." Joseph smiled. "Irene, how are you?"

"I am excellent. The music here is amazing. I knew you played but didn't know I would catch you tonight. This day gets better," I said, smiling. Joseph smiled back.

"I am always on Tuesdays and Sundays. Sit back and enjoy yourself. My uncle and I are about to take the stage. Stay until the end, and I will make it worth it," he said with a wink. *I wonder what he meant by that?*

Voodoo Volume
"Untamed Lust"

Joseph's band, Voodoo Volume, was among the best jazz names ever. I raced to the bathroom and ordered another whiskey before they came on. I stopped checking my watch an hour ago and accepted that tomorrow would be brutal. I was going to maximize fun tonight. I was among those in the crowd cheering the appearance of the band. I took a sip and sat back in anticipation.

Three songs later, I was in love with the exotic sound. It was so unique—instruments foreign to me mixed with the heavenly vocals. The entire trip was worth it for the last two songs alone. I finished clapping. The inside of my hands was red by this point. The scents of cigar smoke now filled the air. I believe I also had a contact high at this point, but I didn't care. I would have to wash my hair in the morning, so be it, because the music I heard was terrific. I was curious why I never heard any other Jazz musicians speak of the band and the music. Why the silence?

Joseph took the mic and spoke, "I would like to thank my friend Irene for coming out today. I am going to dedicate the next song to her. Her father once played these streets with my uncles and father. Give it up to her, her father, and my uncles," he said. The people inside clapped, and I blushed. I didn't know he knew who my father was. I waved to Joseph. This was awesome. "I will play *Untamed Lust* first, then *Hustle of Hucow,* and the final song, *Harem Fertility*. All songs are modified from the original Voodoo hems of our ancestors. This song was passed down for generations in my family. Irene, I hope you enjoy this one."

I settled back in my chair in anticipation of the dedication. Joseph's uncle started the song. The melody was odd and barely sounded like a pattern I recognized. The skill it took to play the song was incredible. I have been playing my entire life, and I didn't think I could play it. This is why I came to New Orleans. This place was magic. I took another sip and savored the flavor. I noticed everyone in the bar was angling to face me and the stage. Odd. I guess they take dedication in the bar seriously. I smiled so much my cheeks were hurting. I didn't know I would be the center of attention at the club when I came.

Joseph blew the horn, and something happened to me. I coughed a couple of times from the sudden feeling. The crowd cheered in response. *Did they know that was going to happen? If so, how?* I looked under the table, and no one was down there. I could have sworn it felt like someone rubbed my clit. Joseph blew the horn again, and I moaned out loud only to slap my mouth with my hand - what the hell was happening? A warmth grew in my body. This is impossible. There isn't any way that a trumpet could do that.

I looked up in utter confusion. Joseph smiled at me and then played more than one note. He blew the horn, cheeks full like a cartoon. I barely saw it. I gripped the table with both hands as the notes danced over my clit. Lady juice gushed like Niagra Falls in my pants. The crowd cheered even more. It felt like two or three tongues were licking my clit, lips, and diving inside my jazz club.

After the initial onslaught, I settled into the feeling. Long, deep breaths fought the cigar smoke for air. Parched lips found the whiskey, and the warmth rose with every note. I tried to smile and play it off, but the people cheered as the musical onslaught danced on my clit. I didn't know how this was happening, but I fully understood that it was happening. Invisible fingers probed my slit — diving and dancing in and out even though I had crossed legs.

The bass rattled my jazzy joystick once more before another tongue licked my ass. I wasn't ready for that, and I moaned loudly. The crowd went wild. Battering with mythical tickles - jolts of energy rushed around my body, combining with excitement. Pricks migrated from my feet toward my midsection to combine into a bomb of lust. *Untamed Lust* was the name of the song, and I understood why. Passion in all forms consumed my body and mind. I couldn't stand, I couldn't walk, I could barely move, as lust cemented me to the chair. I wanted to be fucked more than any other time in my life. I almost drew blood on my lip when I bit it. *Someone, anyone, fuck me right now!*

The music wrapped me in a blanket of warmth and pleasure. I uncrossed my legs in the hopes the feeling would increase or that someone would stop cheering, get up, and ram my wet pussy. Uncrossing my legs helped a little, but the trumpet was the only aspect that increased what was happening. Every note played on the trumpet equally hit a new spot on my body and inside my lady bits. Joseph walked down from the stage toward me. All eyes followed him toward me. He blew the horn, and my response matched.

He blew faster and harder than ever before. I leaned back, trying to fight the orgasm due to sudden embarrassment. Everyone was watching me, cheering, and clapping. I felt exhilarated and humiliated simultaneously but I couldn't fight it any longer. The walls I formed to save me from embarrassment crumbled. The music assaulted my love nookie with every note the pre-orgasm built. Joseph smiled with every blow. One after another, he blew the horn and waited for my reaction.

It felt like it was an extension of him. Joseph was doing this. Was this the lust he had for me? Was it the lust I had for him? Was that the reason it was so intense? I must admit, when I saw him play, I got wet. Was it feeding this? I didn't know what to think. I know what I felt, though. It felt like pure magic inside my sugar walls.

I called out as the vibrations were just too much. I leaned back in the wooden chair, screaming into the music. Joseph played harder, more prolonged, and more intense. It increased the power of my orgasm above anything I had in my life. My entire body shook back and forth. Tears ran down my cheeks from the intensity of the orgasm. The crowd cheered more intensely as I gripped the table and arched my back more. My breast barely stayed inside the dress as I shook from the ripples of pleasure. I was exhilarated and mortified all at the same time. I have never played with myself in front of a boyfriend. Now I just came in front of the club of strangers.

As the song ended, I tried to gather my breath, and the crowd erupted. They stood and cheered for a solid minute before they sat back down. *What the hell do I do now?* I wanted to run and never look back. I also wanted to stay to hear the other two songs. What could happen next? Music had power, and this music had more energy than I thought possible. If I left, could I come back, or would I be seen as someone who couldn't handle the experience? The crowd knew what would happen, and they watched – does this happen often? So many questions. I have to stay. I have to know more, and if that means cumming again, so be it. The last one was fucking awesome.

Hustle of Hucow

Joseph grabbed the mic again. "Give Irene a round of applause." He said, and the crowd went wild. "As everyone knows, the next two songs need two volunteers. Do I have two volunteers? If I do, sit next to Irene," he said. In the darkness of the room, I could see two women stand up and walk over to my table. I thought about getting up and running out of the club. If I did that, I would probably never be able to experience this again. The bar experience is like being scared to go to the local beach, but you go topless when you travel to Spain. Tonight was a once-in-a-lifetime experience, and I was here for it. No matter how wild this gets, I want to experience it, whatever it is.

On either side of me, women sat down. Both had perfect deep brown skin and soulful afros. Large, beautiful mahogany eyes looked at me. Hints of fruity perfume wafted over the smoke of the bar. They smiled, and I felt the warmth. My apprehension dropped. It looks like all three of us will experience the next part together. Good. That made me feel a little better, but I still didn't understand what was coming or who was cumming. One soft touch on my arm and a smile from the woman to my left. I smiled back as the last tremors of my orgasm receded.

The woman on the left spoke, "Amazing, isn't it?"

"Yes, I mean...I didn't know that was possible," I said, responding to Lefty.

"Wait until you hear Hustle of Hucow," said the girl to my right. The smile brought her cheeks high. A warmth radiated from her body, and I felt safe here.

Once again, Joseph's uncle started playing an exotic song. The melody was a genius composition. My body reacted to the song once again. This time, it was different. Hints of tickles slide up and down my rib cage. It felt like ten tongues were sliding, poking, and dancing along my sides and moving upward. My anticipation was palpable. What could be more intense than the previous song? The tickling sensation continued until it centered on my breast. Both of them explode in pleasure. This is new. I never felt anything like it before. *Am I dreaming? This can't be real?*

Lefty looked at me and smiled — one nail placed in her mouth. The devilish grin sent a mild cold chill down my back because I had seen that look on men before. I am not a piece of meat, but she wanted to devour me. I returned the smile to deflect and enjoy the song. Joseph put his lips to the trumpet, and I braced myself. The first tone rushed through my body, and I gasped again for air. Elated that I could experience more, I closed my eyes for a second to hear the song without the misinformation from my eyes. I allowed the song to play for thirty seconds — the rhythm pumping in my veins.

I felt something again, but the feeling was not so easily placed this time. My breast continued to feel amazing, but I could also feel something else from the rest of my body. It was as if pleasure itself ran along my nerves to my nipples from every point on my body. I could feel my heartbeat in my breast — the feeling like that of a thousand tiny needles poking my tits like acupuncture. I opened my eyes when the crowd cheered once more. Both the woman was smiling at me. I moved my hands higher on my breast, and they had enlarged. *What the hell?* The woman to my right giggled at my discovery.

I blushed again, trying to find the words, but I was at a complete loss. I tried to understand what was happening, but I couldn't. My breasts continued to grow, and they pressed against the dress. I became uncomfortable. Joseph played louder and longer. Each time, they grew. I wanted to call out for him to stop before they exploded out of my dress, but I figured that was the point. I came in front of people already. It would hurt to expose myself, too, right?

"It's okay, take them out," said the woman to my right. I turned to look at her while the other woman stood up and walked behind me. I felt her behind me — the warm air blown on the back of the neck. My hair reached for the sky. Goosebumps ran across my shoulders, neck, and chest. Soft lips touched the back of my neck as she caressed my shoulders. The entire time, she spoke words of encouragement as the crowd cheered.

Joseph played louder, and they grew again. The material stretched to the limit. "Can I help you out," she whispered in my ear. I could barely respond in the affirmative because the kisses on the back of my neck confused my emotions. *Was a woman kissing me?* I never even had one of those drunken nights in college when I rubbed nipples with my roommate. Now, a woman was kissing the back of my neck. The soft lips felt so good. I panted from the excitement.

Her fingers searched for the front of my dress while walking over my sensitive breast. With trained precision, the dress was pulled down. I couldn't believe I was in the middle of a jazz club undressing because Joseph played ancient Voodoo songs mixed with jazz. My pink nipples poked out, eager for attention and receiving applause. Beads of milk formed on my exposed nipples. *Am I lactating? How is that possible?*

The woman sitting to my right stood up with intense eagerness. Her thumbs were under the spaghetti straps, and with a quick flick of both hands, the dress fell. Righty was standing in only a blue thong and her high heels. Large, supple breasts as perky as mine stared me in the face. Dark brown nipples that were almost purple moved closer to my face. *Should I suck them? I am not a lesbian, but I want to fuck this woman. Is this the song again, or are my true feelings now reaching the surface?*

The crowd erupted at her disrobing. Joseph hit a high note, and milk squirted out both my nipples. I gasped. The feeling was orgasmic. I smiled wryly at Joseph and focused on the sexual chocolate in front of me. She removed her heels, giving up the five inches they granted her, and put the collection to the side. The blue thong and jewelry were the only things on her body. Righty's fingers found the front of my dress, and she pulled it down. I should stop her. I don't want to be naked in a room full of people. This is like one of those bad dreams when you are naked in front of the class. The crowd clapped and shouted. I lifted my hips, pulling the dress to my ankles. Words of encouragement reigned from the audience. I feed off the excitement, music, and sensuality coming from the woman and let her take my dress and shoes.

The crowd went wild once again. The woman to my right sat on my leg. Long fingers ran along my thigh until they reached my stomach. She was searching and probing along the way until they reached my engorged breast. A subtle squeeze released a little more milk onto her finger. A long tongue licked it from her index finger. She moaned and gazed into my eyes, and that was the moment I realized that I was in trouble.

I moaned again — the pleasure incalculable when Joseph hit more notes that sparked changes in my body. Warmth tickles the outside of my breasts now. The woman behind me moved and sat on my other leg. She must have undressed behind me because she was naked, too. Lefty's chest was more massive than Righty, but her ass was smaller. Each one looked at me, smiling, grabbing, and caressing my body.

Almost in unison, they placed their luscious lips on my nipples and sucked. People have described extreme pleasure before, but I don't know if the most celebrated poet could express the feeling. Joseph played high notes once more. I could feel the hot milk shoot out of my nipples, only to be consumed by the woman. I arched my back to give them a better angle, but my now-massive boobs quickly maneuvered. Lefty preferred to swirl her tongue over the nipple while squeezing with her hands. Righy suckled hard on my nipples and straddled the line of pleasure and pain.

They were good. Each suck and flick felt like my clit. Imagine having two clits, both licked at the same time, by eager and enthusiastic women. Bolts of pleasure raced around my body. They were colliding and hitting with the remnants of the previous orgasm, stacking and building on each other. Milk firing like the prized heifer on the farm I had become. I blushed more; I couldn't believe this was happening to me. I stole a glance at the crowd. Claps and cheers of encouragement ensued. I tried to look at Joseph, but all I could see was hair in that direction, the afros blocking the sightline.

Milk ran down the side of the women's mouths. They sucked, and I squirted. The woman on the left squeezed my breast and slurped one massive gulp. Her mouth was full of my milk. She moved closer. Two hands were placed on the side of my face. A long, deep kiss ensued. I couldn't believe I was kissing a woman, let alone passing sweet milk into my mouth from hers. It tasted delectable and not what I was expecting. Her bare lips were grinding on my leg with increasing speed.

The euphoria came next. The milk was intoxicating. I felt high but without the fogginess. The pleasure increased across my body. Both Righty and Lefty's eyes were glazing over, and it was clear that they felt it, too. The slow grinding on my leg made more sense now as MDMA-like effects kicked in next. The rubbing of my legs felt amazing.

On my other leg, Righty had a little bush, and she was grinding too — both lady bits rubbing on my leg with spilled milk. I giggled. "Don't cry over spilled milk. Fuck it," I said. It was corny, but it popped into my head. Both women briefly laughed and then went back to the regularly scheduled program of sucking my massive shooting breast. Joseph played deep tones, and both women responded. So, I was not the only one affected by the sounds. Both women stopped sucking and ground my legs faster — breasts bouncing in my face. I reached out and grabbed Lefty's larger breast and put her dark nipple into my mouth. I flicked her nipple the same way she flicked my tits, and she smiled, grabbing my head. I was kissing women and sucking tits now, I guess. The crowd roared at the development.

The music sped up, and hints of the first song could be heard under the new song. They both came simultaneously, under the same melody hints that made me come only moments earlier. Joseph was one sneaky bastard. Each one moaned and screamed in the process. I could feel the juices running down my leg, mixing with the spilled milk. Euphoria overcame all three of us as the crowd cheered them on. They kissed long and passionately with each other, my juice running down the side of their mouths.

Once they finished, the attention returned to me. The helpers held the large breast dripping from milk. This time, they didn't drink the milk. They merely held my chest. Joseph played a new variant of the song, and my reaction was instant. I arched my back as a wave of pre-orgasm exploded in my body. What the hell was that? It felt like a man was eating me out for a minute, but instead of feeling it over time, it hit me all at once. It was so intense I couldn't believe such a feeling could exist. Again, he hit me with the exotic notes, and I screamed out this time. The pleasure was overwhelming, and all my inhibitions were gone. I didn't care that anyone was watching me. I was in the middle of the club. The last time he hit the note, I came again.

Both my breasts exploded with milk. It shot out, drenching the two women. That is why they didn't come closer. There is no way they could have swallowed that much Irene juice. Their dark skin covered from the face to the naval. Ropes of hot milk continued to spray them, and they loved it, every second of it with every squeeze of my breath, another ripple of orgasm. The sound was blasting, echoing around the room, and the crowd cheered at a fever level. My chest heaved up and down as the beautiful feeling continued. I can't believe this happened.

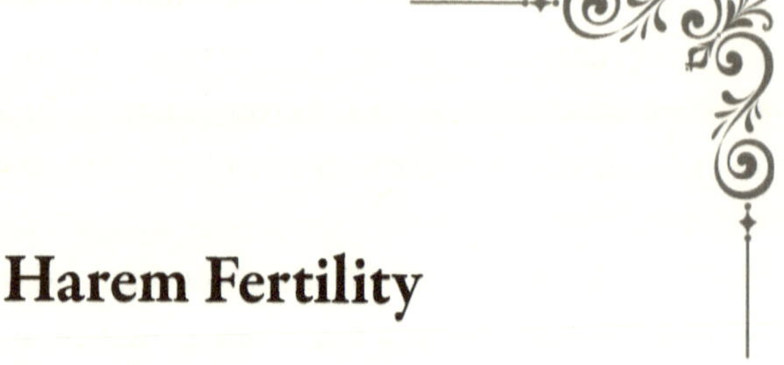

Harem Fertility

Once again, I found myself trying to regain my composure. My heart pounded in my chest loudly, my breast just shot a gallon of milk, and I had orgasmed twice by the sound of music. My mind wondered what life with Joseph would be like. I Imagined him playing a song to make me cum every morning or at night after a hard day at work and in the bath. What other songs did he know? What other pleasures could he inflict? I wanted to know. I didn't know if that was me talking or the song any longer. If you had told me before I arrived that I would have an orgasm from a song, I would say you were crazy, and if you said I would have two beautiful women sucking milk out of my breast before I exploded milk nut on them, I would have told you that you are insane. But it happened.

The next song began. Curiosity and fear were swirling into a cocktail of anticipation. The cocktail intoxicates my every desire, need, and want. I knew what was next but needed to see and experience it. Tingles danced all over my body. It felt like invisible fingers running over my body and touching everywhere but nowhere. The pressure of it didn't exist, but the results were apparent. I moaned once again in my chair. Righty and Lefty cried out, too. I guess it is all three of us simultaneously, but the song did say harem.

Righty and Lefty stood. Lefty pulled me to the table and bent me over. My engorged breast hung, dripping pure white milk on the wood and putting me in a vulnerable position. Seconds later, I felt two-finger slides into me and shortly followed by a tongue flush against my clit.

A woman is eating me out now. Does this make me a lesbian, or do I have to do it too? I couldn't think over the roar of the crowd. Moans of pleasure seemed to come from all directions. The feeling was so exquisite and dirty. In between groans, I took deep breaths of the cigar smoke bar.

Righty walked in front of the table, and Joseph walked down to the table from the stage. He was mere feet from my naked body. My eyes told him a story. You're the reason why this is happening to me. If you had left me alone in that bar, I wouldn't be here. I wouldn't be cumming in front of strangers. I wouldn't be milked like a human cow. I wouldn't have lovely ebony fingers plunging ever deeper inside me. You're the reason for all of this, and I thank you.

Righty bent down and unzipped his pants. A monster cock almost the size of his trumpet plopped out and proliferated. I wondered if his songs had the same effect on him that he did on my breast because that was the largest cock I had seen. Veins rippled around the dark cock, now glistening from the spit left by Righty's mouth. Steady hand movement brought his instrument to attention. I licked my lips, watching her suck that cock. Spit hung from her chin down to her breast. I wanted it. I wanted all of it. Joseph put that in my mouth, too.

Lefty pushed me flat onto the table and then flipped me onto my back. She hopped on top of me, kissing me and mingling my juices inside my mouth. She pulled back and giggled, looking into my eyes.

"This is going to be fun. I was the honored guest last month," she said. "As you can see, I came back for more."

"Do you come here often," was all I could manage between kisses. I guess you have to at least talk to someone that just fingerfucked you sticky and licked your clit.

"No, I am an accountant from New York. My name is Rasheeda. That's Latifah from St. Louis. We come here occasionally to escape," she said, smiling. They were just like me. Escaping life for this, but what was this? Rasheeda's eyes went wide. I felt her sliding on top of me, tit to tit.

She moaned, "Fuck, that's a big cock."I leaned to the side and saw his hips. Joseph was fucking her.

I could see him still playing his instrument while the crowd erupted. She moaned out loudly. I could hear the smacking of his hips on her ass. I smacked her ass once and smiled. With each stroke, she let out a moan. I understand why. Joseph was splitting her in two with the monster and making her cum with the song. The fact he could do that and still play was utterly unique. Rasheeda was getting destroyed from behind doggy style while my pussy was mere inches from her in missionary.

In the middle of my pondering about how long he trained to fuck and play the horn, I felt something substantial pressing against my lips. Rasheeda kissed my neck and moaned as the giant cock tried to get inside my tight lips. The mushroom was larger than any vibrator, dildo, or sex toy I had seen on the market, let alone on a man. He blew the horn, and I could feel my lips spread more. Holy shit, I was getting fucked by that monster.

I should tell him to stop. I should run out of the bar and never come back. That is what I should do. What I am doing is letting Rasheeda kiss my neck, allow the unprotected monster inside, and enjoy this. Joseph played the subtle notes that tickled her clit. I am also sucking Latifa's nipple now, leaking milk like mine was before. I could see the rapid growth of her breast now overcome by the subtle notes of the hucow song. The euphoria-inducing milk sparked more pleasure as a foot-long cock with the girth of a soda can slid inside.

It disappeared into my shaven pink pussy before Latifa's hucow tits sprayed milk on me. My lady juice covered his cock, trying to provide the lube needed to fuck such a tight cunt. I was getting covered by the creamy milk and stretched all at the same time. The milk tingled on the exposed skin, inside my mouth, on my breast, and now on my pussy as she drenched me.

The music went insane as all three songs meshed. Rasheeda exploded into orgasm under the wild sounds. Her cries of pleasure are now mixing with the music. Cheers from the audience combined with her shaking body. She squeezed me hard as my lips squeezed the instrument deep inside my pussy. Joseph continued to play his trumpet as his other horn worked my pussy. Rasheeda started to suck the milk from Latifa. Latifa sat on my face, her pussy inches away, the excess fluid running down her body falling on my face.

Joseph sped up the pace of the song and his long strokes. Latifa came. Milk shot all over me, Rasheeda, and Joseph—the blast covered the entire table. Ropes continued to shoot out as she shuttered from the expenditure. My whole body tingled from the liquid, and now I understood why they let me soak them before. I wasn't high, and I wasn't drunk, but I was something. The feeling was more like that of Molly or Excatasy than high I felt. Thousands of fingers seemed to touch my skin in the way I like. Nothing but pleasure and a little pain from the monster cock now moving much faster in and out. It delighted my insides, undoubtedly the by-product of a note or key I couldn't recognize them.

I didn't need the song that made me and Rasheeda cum earlier. The dick was enough. I exploded at the same time he did. I spasmed and shook on the slick table as hot ropes of cum shot almost directly into my womb because the cock was so deep inside me. The crowd went wild. Their energy feeds into me cum like a wave of energy. Joseph put the trumpet down, grabbed both my legs, and pounded every last drop of his seed into me. I gasped out, moaning loudly and yelling. He pulled it out, and hot cream spilled onto the floor. I put my legs down and hung off the side of the table. I looked at Rasheeda and smiled; she was lying beside me doing the same thing.

The alarm went off the next day. I rolled over slowly, piecing together the rest of the night. Latifah, Rasheeda, Joseph, and I were drenched in milk. We took our discarded clothing and went to the shower in the back. Playfully we washed each other, enjoying the escape, the milk, and the cock. I stumbled back to the hotel and collapsed into bed. It now felt like I had ten jackhammers in my head. The pain between my legs felt like eighteen bulldozers rammed into my pussy the night before. I could barely walk from the Mandigo Backbreaker. I usually wear heels everywhere, but I must wear sandals today. Three people asked me if I was okay and hurt, and I waved them off. *I am okay, and* I told everyone that.

It wasn't until I saw a pregnant woman at the conference did I remember I was turned into a cumdumpster by Joseph. *I might be pregnant!* I saw Rasheeda in the corner, slowly sipping a coffee. After a moment, I was finally able to get her attention. She laughed and pointed to the corner. I looked to the corner and saw Latifah struggling to stay awake. I laughed to myself, retired to my room, contemplated how I would go on living and fell asleep.

Intruder: White Female Police Officer Plays Cops & Robbers

By: Racheal Darkside

The garage door closed behind me, and I breathed a sigh of relief. I am home—a long shift during another round of protests frays the nerves. If it isn't the libs, then it is the conservatives. Both sides piss me off now. Plus, I didn't have to cry after the protest. Sometimes, the abuse I take from the protestors rushes back after the adrenaline dump. A callus formed in my heart that I hope will go away one day. My husband is one promotion away from retiring me to a consulting life. The man is breaking his back, so I won't have to endure this anymore. Did I mention he is the best?

I sit for five, ten, and sometimes even twenty minutes every time I get home. The simple moment allows for the transformation from Police Sargent to Cindy, the wife and mom of two. I need to calm my nerves, or I will snap at everyone. My husband, the best human on this planet, gives me the space and time to do so. Give is not the word. He told me to wait at least five minutes and to take more time if needed. The thought of my husband triggers the waterworks in my eyes. He is not home, and the only thing I want to do is to take a shower and snuggle with him. I wiped the tear, and the water made a clean streak on the dirty fingers.

I took those five minutes of zen even though no one was home. When you have a regiment, it is essential to continue it. I jumped out of the SUV and punched the code. The friendly tone alerted me that the door was ready, and I opened the door. On the other side, a gym bag for dirty clothing. I can shower after my shift but wanted to be in my castle today. During COVID, I ensured I didn't bring it home with me. I also drop my clothes from the station and place them into the bag. They go straight to the washing machine once the bag is full.

The home was quiet and dark. My husband took the kids to his mother's place on the other side of the city. I could have worked overtime, so he took the kids. The ground floor of the row home was an entertainment room, bathroom, and small office. I shut the door behind me and listened for people. Sometimes, my husband likes to surprise me, I miss the text when plans change, or something like that. One time, my brother-in-law almost got an eye full when I got home during the end of COVID.

I took the bag into the bathroom. The small bathroom was a primarily white minimalist modern design. My bathroom, full of all the beauty products, made me feel like a woman. I put my service weapon alongside my handcuffs, cell phone, and badge on the vanity. In this process, I stripped my police clothing and put it in the bag. I physically removed the clothing and stared at my body in the mirror. My breasts weren't as perky as they once were, but still lovely. The training allowed for the maintenance of muscles, tone, and a killer six-pack. I hoped that was enough to keep my husband. We were the model for what women were looking for. The man devil is over six feet tall, over six figures, and over six inches tall. Women practically throw themselves over him whenever they go out together. I grabbed the phone and thought about taking a picture to send to him, but I wasn't feeling that sexy yet. Maybe I will be in the mood after the shower and two hours of romantic comedies.

I took a long and hot shower in the dark. I liked it that way. Only the nightlight provides illumination in the room. Not only did I wash away the dirt and grime from the day, but the stimulus. Listening to people scream over the bullhorn for ten hours will give you a headache. I would trade the noise for the noise of my kids playing and my husband turning up the volume to hear the football game. Speaking of families, I have barely seen mine in a long time, and I wonder if my husband still wants me. I spiral into a depression, and I almost fall into the hole before I catch myself. *Get it together, Cindy, go inside, see your husband when this is over, and he still wants you.* I would love to see him, but he took the kids to the other side of town. I almost cry again because I want him home. I want to be in his arms while he squeezes me.

I Heard A Sound

After the purge, I stepped out of the shower and thought I heard a noise. I walked past the towel and grabbed my gun. I was naked and vulnerable, everything I hated in this world. The last thing I wanted to do was get caught drying my hair as that asshole tossed me to the ground and had his way with me. After I scanned the entertainment room, I slid back into the bathroom to grab my phone and cuffs. Slowly, I gathered a plain white cotton tank top and short grey shorts at the base of the stairs. I put them on quickly and put my blond hair in a mom bun.

I walk up the stairs slowly, trying not to make a sound. When I reached the top of the stairs, I heard a noise. I wasn't imagining the sound. Someone was in the rowhome. Something is off. The light in the backroom was one, and it shuns into the kitchen. The open design wouldn't hide my approach for much longer. My adrenaline spiked, and I slowly maneuvered around the corner, ready to confront anything I saw. Someone entered the kitchen and opened the refrigerator, taking out food and putting it into a gym bag.

"Freeze," I yelled. I couldn't see much in the darkness; that light was still off, but the light from the refrigerator created a large outline. The man was big, so I took another step back. Someone his size could cover the distance between us faster than you think. I yelled again for him to stop what he was doing. The adrenaline pumped in my veins, and I took off my safety but kept my finger off the trigger.

"Hands up. That's a right, nice and slow asshole," I said. I looked around for a place to put the mountain of man before seeing how much smaller I was and decided he wanted to test me. I am not the biggest person in the world, but what I lack in size, I make up in tenacity. My grandfather, dad, uncle, and two brothers are all cops. Unlike them, I am not over six feet tall and two hundred and twenty pounds. In my dad's infinite wisdom, my dad decided to marry a five-foot-tall woman; in turn, I am five foot-four. I love superhero movies like anyone else, but a 115-pound woman can't knock out what looked to be a six-foot-three-man in the real world. If he got to me before I put him down, it would not end well for me.

"Sit down on the chair and put your hands behind your back," I command. The man walks over to the chair and sits down. He tried to speak, but I shut him up. The monster sat in the chair, put his hands behind his back, and threw the bars in the chair. The further we got from the fridge, the harder it was to see, and I feared I would lose him in the darkness. The light from the street coming through a sliver in one window had to be enough.

I move behind him. "Move, and I shoot," I warned. I latched the first wrist quickly and then the second with my gun trained on his back. He could if this monster wanted to get out, but it would take a few seconds. I put the safety on my gun and set it down. The mountain wore a sweatshirt and grey sweatpants. I pat down his pockets and find a wallet. I take the wallet from the sweatpants, open it, and look at the driver's license.

Rahiem Woods

"Hello, Rahiem Woods. Is there any reason you decided to come to my house and steal my food? You know what? I don't care. I can't wait to see what the boys at the precinct do with you for breaking into a cop's house. I imagine they will claim you struggled. Rahiem, Rahiem, Rahiem, this is not good," I said.

"Fuck you, cop. We are starving out here," he growled. "Call your goons. They don't scare me. My hungry children are scarier than those goons."

They all say that until the boys stop by, and then they sing a different toon. I continued to search for weapons, and I felt something. I reach into his pocket and touch something, but it seems it's tucked into his waistband. I reach into his waistband. It was thick and hard. Maybe it was a flashlight or something long and hard to club me with. Thankfully, it wasn't a gun. I tried to take it, but I couldn't free it. Every time I pulled, it stayed in place.

"I guess little white girls like you have never felt a true blood Alabama Black Snake. That's right, pig. Keep stroking that black snake girl," he snickered.

"That's not your cock, asshole. That's a flashlight or something. Where is it connected?" I respond. I pulled down his waistband and reached inside. I gripped the object—my little hand pulled on it. I could feel the skin of the item, and I smiled. The robber was rock hard. It is indeed a cock—an Alabama Black Snake. Curious, I ran my hand from the bottom to the tip and couldn't believe how big it was. I need to see this thing. I stepped away and turned on the light.

Rahiem was snickering at my gaze. The Alabama Black Snake twitched under his command. I wanted a better look, so I pulled his sweatpants to his ankles. I grab it again and feel the warm cock. My hand couldn't even fit around the monster. The dark black cock contrasted against my pale skin.

I pulled his shirt up a little to expose rock-hard abs, and for the first time, I looked at his face. The man was gorgeous, and I got a sudden rush of emotion. My little cop cookie exploded with juices, and for the first time in a long time, I was in charge, not the damn protestors. I could do whatever I wanted to Rahiem and get away with it. I could call the boys and have him arrested or play with him a little, let him go, and satisfy what I was missing. I hadn't seen a cock in ten days, and my lips, both of them, were moist thinking about it inside.

"Don't take this the wrong way, Rahiem. But you are a good-looking man with an amazing cock." I said. "Maybe I just," and let the rest of the sentence trail off as my hand slid up and down the shaft.

"I guess we could help each other out," he smirked.

Let's Make a Deal

"**G**ood decision, Rahiem. Now let's investigate this Alabama Black Snake of yours," I said, getting to one knee and inspecting the eleven inches. Not only was it big, but it was thick. I poked it with my finger. It moved a little and then snapped to attention like a recruit. I could feel the weight of it with the pressing finger. I stuck my tongue out and licked it. The cock was fresh. I opened my mouth as wide as it could and barely fit over the helmet. It smelled like cocoa butter and cologne. Delicious. This man knows what he is doing. I pull back to admire once again. This time, the helmet glistened from my spit.

The intruder eggplant was a two-hander, so my left hand gripped the base, and my right hand gripped the top. Each time down, I went a little farther and filled my mouth with a snake. I pulled back and licked his balls while stroking the mighty monster. I focused on it as if nothing else existed in the world.

I notice a splash of white at the tip—a little precum beaded. I was trying to decide how nasty I would get with the criminal, but my primal urges were already peaked, so I licked it off. I am such a naughty girl, but I could get naughtier. I devoured the head after, pulling back and creating a popping sound. My lady bits exploded by my exploits. My inner slut was hungry, and it ate like it was slut Thanksgiving.

I stopped the cock worship and pulled down my shorts. Rahiem smirked, so I slapped his cock. "What is so funny, Rahiem?"

"I don't think it will fit, officer," he said. "It looks like your hole is too small. Are you sure you can take this?"

I held the base and smacked the cock again. The intruder yelped. I held my hand next to it and looked at it, "Keep talking, and I start smacking balls next. Do you want that?" The control fed my desire. My emotions spiked, and my arousal increased to a fearful pace. I am in control here, buddy. Nothing you say or do will change that.

"No," he said. I smacked his balls anyway. I thought my directions were clear, but some people are slow learners. "Damn, bitch."

"Bitch," I smacked his balls and hard cock once more. "Bad snake." I held my hand like I would beat it again and looked at him. This time, he didn't say a word.

"You don't get to talk. I am in control here. You sit there. Understand," I ordered. I was testing to see if he understood the rules. Rahiem nodded in agreement, and this time, I smirked. "Good job Rahiem. You are such a quick learner." Then I smacked it again, and he grunted but didn't talk. I smiled and got on my knees again.

I again put the monster helmet into my mouth, savoring the flavor. My hands crept lower, eager to join, but this meant I only had one hand for the Alabama Black Snake, but I believed I could manage. My fingers found my eager lady bits. He was right about one thing: it didn't look like it would fit, but it would. I had to warm the old girl up first.

My fingers plunged inside. I was dripping wet. I could hear the squishing sound as I played with myself. I had to gasp a couple of times while slobbering. My body was on fire with desire, but I had to ensure we were ready to receive the monster.

"Do you have a girlfriend, hookup, or wife?" I asked. I wanted to know who claimed this thing.

"Wife," he said, and then I smacked his cock again. I then kissed the spot and made it better.

"Your wife would hate what is about to happen," I said, standing up. My fingers were dripping wet from my lips. I thought getting wet would take a few minutes, but I was dripping. For the first time in a while, I was in control. Also, I was going to fuck a cock.

"I bet your wife is sexy. You are a handsome man. I wish she could watch me fuck her cock. She would be pissed," I said. I had to get as high as possible on my tippy-toes to align the Alabama Black Snake. I straddle him on the chair, hoping to align it right. If I slipped and this thing went into my ass, I may never walk again.

I lowered myself onto it and felt my dripping wet cop cookie crumble. I watched the dark chocolate go inside my vanilla ice cream. The warm cock stretched my neglected nana for a good thirty seconds to get the tip inside. I let out a moan and a couple of curses. Shit. He was thick. My little girl kept expanding and taking on the challenge. I rocked up and down. Each time, I was able to get more of it inside. I moaned from the extreme pleasure the giant cock provided.

The helmet was hitting parts of my vagina that hadn't been touched in some time. "Damn, Rahiem, this is good shit. Fuck. I bet your wife would be pissed if she knew a dirty cop tamed this Alabama Black Snake. My husband has a nice cock, but nothing like this," I said, sliding down the furthest yet. The cock was slick enough to ride it.

I took my tank top off because it was chaffing my nipples. I pressed my girls against his muscular chest. The warmth from his body heated mine. I pushed back, and I could lift my toes off the ground for the first time. I was riding him on the chair because it was deep enough. I was moaning, grunting, and making sounds like people speaking in tongues. I leaned forward again, grabbed his head, and pushed it into my breast. I picked up the pace, using his head as the lever, and felt the black snake drive my insides wild. I love it. I love being in control.

"You like this pussy, don't you. You can't get enough of this white pussy," I taunted. "Don't you dare cum in me? I am not on birth control, and my husband and I are trying to have a baby."

"Are you," he responded. I smacked him in the face and then kept riding. It felt so good. I rode the entire shaft from the balls to the tip.

"No talking. Like I said, my husband and I are trying to have a baby, so don't you dare cum inside me. He doesn't know it yet, but we are. I don't want you cumming inside me and ruining it. I am just going to ride it a little longer. I am about to cum. Also, if you cum before I do, I am calling the boys. You don't get off unless I get off. Don't you dare cum inside me? Hold it," I ordered.

I sped up, knowing he was close to cumming. I wanted to cum before he did. The race was on. I continued to tell him not cum as I rode him. I couldn't get off until I did. The cock felt so good—the pleasure and pain of it. Sometimes, it was going too far inside, and it hurt. Sometimes it would batter my gspot and bring the orgasm one step closer. Either way, I enjoyed it all: the control and the power I had over him. I didn't want it to stop. Once it ended, I had to think about the protest again. Nope, but two pump chump over here had a time limit.

"That's it, that's it, just one more second," I said. I bounced faster and faster on my spot. One hand on my clit rubbing furiously and the other on his shoulder guiding my frantic bouncing. Then I came with the full force of a stressed-out cop without her husband's touch for ten days. The Alabama Black Snake also had enough. It spits venom inside me. The sudden warmth I believed to be my orgasm running its course, but it wasn't. I could feel the massive snake dumping inside mc. Each rope of cum seemed to align with a wave of orgasm. Damn, that was good cock.

It was so warm, and it filled me like a twinkie. I leaned forward and put my head on his shoulder, out of breath even as the last ropes of the Alabama black snake's hot venom filled me up. When he finished, I put both hands on his shoulder and rocked back and forth on the still rock-hard cock. Rahiem twitched from riding on his sensitive post cum cock.

"I thought I told you, Rahiem Woods, not to cum inside me?"

"I thought I heard officer Cindy Woods say that she wanted to get pregnant by her husband," he said. I leaned forward and kissed him. The embrace probably only lasted a few seconds but felt much longer. "What are you doing? How are the kids?"

Rahiem smiled, "The kids wanted those damn snacks, and the store was out. I knew we had some, and I thought I could come in and get them and get out. We haven't played cops and robbers in a while. We need to bring that back. Next time, the robber wins," he said with a smile.

"How are you doing? I know it has to be hard for you, babe. The overtime is good when the check comes, but I miss you," he said. I reached around the chair and unlocked the handcuffs, and he hugged me. I squeezed him tight, and I started crying. I sat on top of him with the black snake inside until he went limp. I don't know if it lasted a minute, an hour, or a day, but the embrace was everything I needed.

The silence ended when he spoke, "I don't care what you see. I love you. I know it is hard for both of us. I know you hear things that make you upset. I am here for you, always and forever. You hear me. Always. I am bringing the family back tomorrow. You need us, and we need you," he said. I pulled back with a mountain of tears and kissed him. "That's tomorrow. Now I need you to go back downstairs and come back up. This time, the thug wins. Your mom can watch the kids a little bit longer without you."

I wiped the tears away, kissed him, and got dressed. I raced down the stairs, and he turned off all the lights. I walked up the stairs, and he rushed me in the dark. I fought back, but I couldn't win against him. My lady bits exploded with juice again and was eager to take on the Alabama blacksnake again. My face pressed into granite on the island, my clothes were torn, and my body ached from the intensity. "Black cocks matter," he teased. My husband pounds me until he deposits another monster load inside me, and that was only after I came two more times. I love that man, and we are now expecting.

Mistaken Identity: I didn't know she had a BBC!

By: Toi La Boi

I couldn't remember the last time I was this horny. Young college men with rippling muscles, veiny forearms, and exposed bulges took over her house. Her daughter's college friends didn't seem to like clothing either. The women flaunted young perky breasts as they bounced around in the slutty version of every profession known to man. This year's drunkgiving occurred at my house, and the young adults decided to have a costume theme. I didn't even know you could make a slutty version of baby shark, but I watched a black-haired friend of my daughter twerk in the costume. The sexual tension pulsated in the room, and Janet wasn't spared from its devilish pull.

I smiled at her daughter and her girlfriend in the corner. My daughter was just like me. We were both the same height, not petite, but not a giant. On the other hand, my daughter's girlfriend was tall. The tall woman wore the Wonder Woman costume, and my daughter wore the same Slave Leia costume I had on. Keke wore a Wonder Woman costume with high boots. She had bare shoulders, a fit body, a short skirt, and long black hair. The outfit exposed her dark brown skin that seemed to glow a golden hue.

When they started dating, I didn't know how to feel about it. I sent my daughter to college, and she returned with a nice boy. I thought she found her prince charming. He was a tall boy with blond hair and blue eyes. A year later, he was out of the picture and was replaced by Keke.

I was mad at first, but after she talked about how happy she was all the time, I felt better about it.

One thing was for sure. The party boasted my self-esteem. I was apprehensive about wearing the outfit as my daughter, but she insisted. Her words, "Mom, you slay." The young men noticed my hot milf body, and I soaked up the attention. I remained for ten minutes before my drink ran out.

I went up the stairs to make another drink and to stop these young and horny adults from having sex around my house. I went to the kitchen and poured my drink from the hidden stash. The college kids would drink the cheap stuff that would give me a hangover for a week. My daughter left her bag on the floor, so I picked it up and went up the stairs.

When I made it up the stairs, I heard the first noises. The bathroom door was shut, and when I walked to the door and felt the handle, the door was locked. I heard a woman cursing up a storm. The slapping sounds were fast. Damn, she was getting pounded. I was mad because I knew I wouldn't touch anything in the house until the cleaners came, but it also made me hornier than these college sluts. I caught myself as I touched my naughty bits.

I almost stopped in my room and got my vibrator, but I remembered my daughter's bag. I also needed to check the other rooms. Having sex in the bathroom was one thing, but I didn't want anyone skeet-skeeting from the windows to the walls. The three guest rooms on the floor were clear for the moment. I went to the fourth room, my daughter's room, and placed her bag on the counter. She then went to her daughter's closet and slid the door open. It was dark because she didn't turn on the lights. The two would steal each other's clothing often enough that she knew where it went.

Suprise

I felt hands wrap around her body and kiss my neck. The kisses were furious, and the tongue quickly explored her ear lobes. A hand gripped my mouth, and I moaned slightly. I guess my husband was as horny as I was, but he wasn't supposed to guard the basement. The last time she saw him, the older was doing a keg stand. I thought he would be passed out by now, but I guess the crazy sexual energy inspired him, too. The fire and fury of his hands were unforgettable. Janet hasn't felt this level of passion for some time.

The cosplay top was easy to circumvent, and one hand gripped my breast and flicked my nipple. The other hand went under the slave flap and played eagerly with my lady bits. I was dripping wet in less than a minute before a hand descended downstairs. I closed my eyes and embraced the passion of the moment. My husband was fired up, and I felt raging passion for the first time in a long time.

The hand only worked for a moment before the tip of a cock pressed against my lips. The hard cock went inside with ease. I was a torrent of party juices and a favorite. I moaned in pleasure. My wet insides gripped the thick meat. *Huh*, I thought. *When did my husband's cock get this big? When did he take his boner pills? How was he even this hard after drinking?*

I didn't need the answer right now because the extra hard cock was everything I wanted and needed at that moment. The long strokes touched all the places that needed attention. I braced against the wall of the closet and felt the power of his hips. The long strokes seemed to go deeper and deeper than before. Janet cursed because his stamina tonight was terrific. The smack of my ass startled me for a moment. My husband wasn't allowed to do that. Maybe he was overcome with the same passion that I was, or he was too drunk. It didn't matter. On Tuesday, I would rip him a new asshole for smacking my ass, but he would get a pass during the hedonistic drunkgiving party.

He took the cock out and grabbed Janet's hair. The mighty man directed the cock into her mouth. Sucking his penis after it was inside was a big no-no for me. Before I could protest, I tasted myself and the thick cock. My husband's face fucked me hard. Spit dripped down my chin and onto the floor like a good little slut. The ramming didn't stop for a minute before he took it out.

"Take that, Juile. You have been such an asshole today. Is this why? Did you want to piss me off to make sure I rammed you? Well, here it is," SHE said, pulling me from the ground. Oh fuck. This isn't my husband. It is my daughter's girlfriend. A girlfriend that I just found out had an excellent penis.

I reached out and felt the Wonder Woman costume skirt. I opened my eyes and took in the sight with the small amount of light. My head was down, and all I could see was the wedges. Keke wore the white toenail polish. The cock gagged me again before I could catch her breath. Keke continued to berate me for my daughter's behavior that day. I knew very well how much of an asshole Julie could be and imagined Julie pushed Keke to the limit. I needed to stop this before it went any further. It was an honest mistake for both of us. She thought I was my daughter, who wore the same outfit, and I thought she was my husband because of her size and strength. We could step apart, agree never to speak of it again, and go our separate ways. If I did that, on the other hand, I would not get that hard and thick big black cock again. My inner good girl told me to stop, but my inner ho told me to continue. I agreed to a compromise. I would let it go on a little longer, feel that cock one more time, and then push her away.

Once again, I was pressed against the wall. This time the fire and furious futa cock reached for the back of my love whole. In a way, this was my husband's fault. He was the one who made the bet that brought me to the place. The bet, when my daughter and I lost, was to wear the same outfit. Even though my daughter said my body was *slay*, she didn't want to do it. He threatened to cancel the party if she didn't wear it. Janet's husband made a bet with the two of them that they lost. The punishment was to wear the same outfit for the party. We both had flowy blond hair, were the same height, and threw a lot of effort on my part, the same build. That wasn't her husband's cock but her daughter's girlfriend's cock.

I had no idea her daughter's girlfriend was trans, trap, futa, or whatever, for starters, but her cock was amazing. She isn't the cheating type and would never have pursued it, but she understood why people cheated now. Her husband is older, and it is hard for them to be romantic. Her lady bits screamed for her to continue, and her brain tried to pull them away from the nice cock.

I cursed internally. My daughter was getting this cock routinely, and she had the nerve to start fights with the person it was attached to. She clearly didn't understand how good this was. I allowed it to continue a little longer. I had the mother of all orgasms building. After I was satisfied, I would turn around and end it. There was simply nothing to gain by stopping it before then. The cock already went into my mouth, and slave Leia snatch. Stopping it now would only deny an amazing orgasm and would leave me hornier than before.

I told myself I deserved this, and it was my husband's fault. If it had not made them wear the same outfit, this would not be happening. The sex was also my reward for running three times a week and eating like a gerbil. Why not have a young stallion? The hard work allowed a twenty-one-year-old with a thickie to pound the nookie. The sinister grin reflected the dark place the mind wandered. My lust was untamed, unmatched, and unnatural for the moment.

The young woman clamped her hands on my hips and pounded as hard as she could. When I was younger, I would hate it when the young boys jackhammered the juicy vajayjay. Now, I would pay for a thrashing like this. Thankfully, I didn't have to. The length of her junk went all the way in, then out, until the tip barely stayed inside before pounding again.

Her hand went to my clit, and she rubbed furiously. The right leg shook, the first sign of the impending explosion. I felt the damn breaking cracks of euphoria poured into my body. I smiled deviously during the process. The other leg wiggled, and I came furiously. Waves of pleasure consumed my body like a fire. I loved it. The cock was terrific, and I felt great.

I wasn't the only one that came. The jackhammering Johnson exploded hot young trap sauce inside my taco. I cursed in pleasure as the warmth tickled my orgasm. The seemingly never-ending torrent of cum filled me to the brim. That is when I remembered a little fun fact. I wasn't on birth control because my husband had a vasectomy years ago. The young futa firehouse continued to dump its contents inside of me. At the moment, she didn't care. The orgasms turned my insides into a raging inferno of lust.

"Damn, Janet, that was amazing," Keke said. My name is Janet. Shit, she knew.

"Keke? I thought you were my husband," I pretended.

"Okay, yeah, right. I saw your husband's package. You knew. By the way, you were eye fucking me all night. I knew you wanted a taste. Oh, and how couldn't you know when you sucking it. When I saw you down there taking it like a champ, I wanted to make sure to give you the fuck that you wanted," said Keke.

Keke took a step back, and my eyes were on the mighty young cock as it dripped under the skirt. I marveled at the juices and wanted to get on her nasty knees to clean it off, but women of polite society do not do such things. We both came so much that it was drenched. Keke looked down at it and chuckled at the unsaid observations. The two stared at each other for about thirty seconds, neither speaking. I played the surprise to the extent that she would bring it home.

"Okay. Listen up," I said. The cheating cougar took control and grabbed my chest. "You say nothing, and I say nothing. Got it. Oh, and never cum in my daughter again. I don't care what she says. Cum on her ass, tits, on her face. I don't care. Also, that was fucking amazing. Thanks, Keke. You fucking rock. Don't ever cheat on my daughter again, or I will cut off your cock and balls, stuff it, and use it as a dildo for the rest of my lie," I said. I leaned in and kissed Keke on the cheek, smacked her ass, and retired to my room to take a shower.

My husband passed out on the bed when I got out of the shower. I wanted a round two and thought getting another load that night would be fun, but he wouldn't work now. I went downstairs wearing night clothing and watched the party die and stop. The following day, I got up in the best mood of my life, made breakfast for all the young adults, and talked. Eventually, they left, but Keke stayed. Though I promised that I never was going to do it again, I couldn't help myself, and Keke and I had sex three more times, and each time, she exploded inside of me. Somehow, I dodged being pregnant. When my daughter called me three weeks later and said Keke wasn't coming to the house for the holidays because she was a cheating bitch, I almost cried. I was looking forward to her cock again. After the holidays, I received a text from Keke. She wanted to meet up, and I was on my way.